COMIC CHAPTER BOOKS

DC COMICS SUPER HEROES

# BATMAN



STONE ARCH BOOKS
a capstone imprint

Batman: Comic Chapter Books are published by
Stone Arch Books,
A Capstone Imprint
1710 Roe Crest Drive
North Mankato, Minnesota 56003
www.capstonepub.com



Star33638



Cataloging-in-Publication data is available on the Library of Congress website

ISBN: 978-1-4965-0513-2 (library binding)
ISBN: 978-1-4965-0515-6 (paperback
ISBN: 978-1-4965-2304-4 (eBook)

Summary: Bruce Wayne is in the rainforests of Brazil, but there's trouble in the local villages — people are disappearing! Corporate developers are tearing down the forest, and a legend tells of a giant bat creature that will defend the plant life from those who would destroy it. Batman takes up the case, and he soon finds out the strange goings-on are more than just folklore — it's Man-Bat and Poison Ivy!

Printed in Canada.
052015 008825FRF15

COMIC CHAPTER BOOKS

DC COMICS™ SUPER HEROES

# BATMAN™

## ATTACK OF THE MAN-BAT!


Batman created by Bob Kane

written by
Jake Black

illustrated by
Luciano Vecchio

# TABLE OF CONTENTS

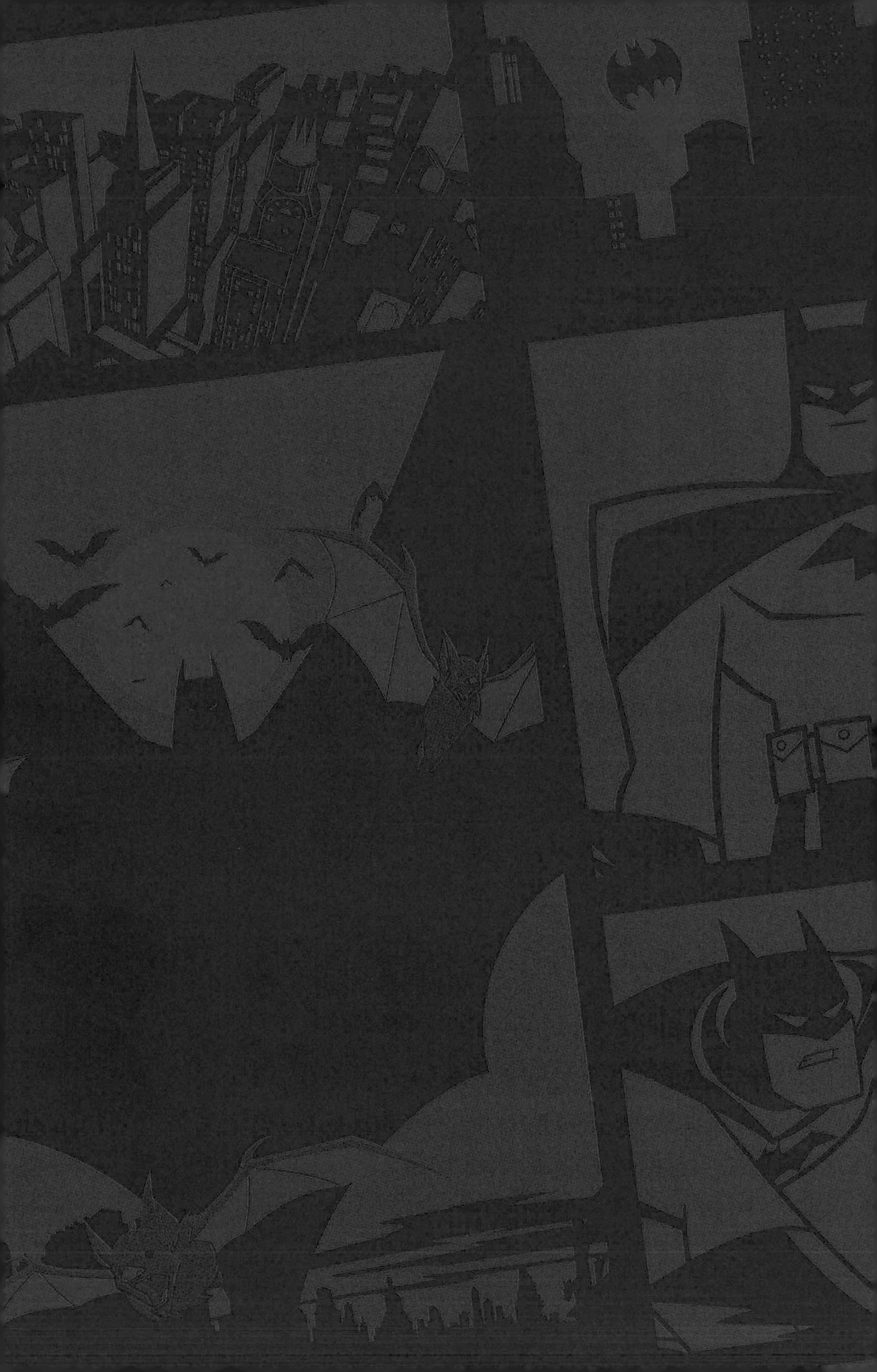

CHAPTER 1

# DISAPPEARING

Bruce Wayne hated these types of meetings. Whenever rich businessmen got together, all they did was brag about the money they made and the power they had. The endless posturing made it hard to talk about anything that was actually important.

At least this time the scenery was beautiful. The World Congress of Economic Leaders was gathered in a large auditorium in the middle of the rainforest region of Brazil. Their meeting was supposed to be about environmental protections.

But as usual, the meeting had turned into a bragging game, which meant they likely wouldn't make any deals to better the world — just to better their own personal incomes and stock portfolios.

An oil executive took to the podium. He boasted about the success he'd had — fast cars, a large mansion, and expensive clothes.

Bruce sighed. *Where was the discussion of bettering the world?* he wondered.

"Are you as bored as I am, Ms. Pantozzi?" Bruce asked the businesswoman sitting next to him.

She smiled. "You know it, Bruce," she said. "Somehow I don't think we're going to save the world today."

Bruce smiled back. "No," he said. "That's later in the week. That is, if we can get them to listen to anything we have to say."

Bruce had asked Ms. Pantozzi to accompany him on this trip because she was the executive in charge of environmental protections for Wayne Enterprises. No one at Wayne Enterprises knew more about saving the planet than Ms. Pantozzi did.

Together, Bruce and Ms. Pantozzi had developed a plan that would help preserve the rainforest. It was detailed and budgeted efficiently and entirely reasonable. They'd worked long and hard to get every detail right.

They were supposed to present the plan to the group at the end of the conference, two days from now. Bruce was hopeful that his colleagues and friends at the conference would join with them in the plan. With their support, the conservation program would be a big success.

Bruce had his doubts they'd take an interest, though.

Suddenly the speaker's boasting was interrupted by a group of protesters bursting into the back of the auditorium. They carried signs that read: "Protect the Rainforest!," "Earth First!," and "Love Mother Earth!"

SAVE OUR PLANET!
SAVE THE RAINFOREST!
PLEASE SAVE MY HUSBAND! THE GIANT BAT MONSTER TOOK HIM!
BAT MONSTER...?
PLEASE! THE BAT MONSTER, IT--

Bruce watched as security guards forced the protesters out of the building. He was concerned. These types of protests almost always happened at such meetings.

But this time, Bruce was particularly concerned for one special reason: a protester had screamed about a giant bat monster.

*What could it mean?* he thought.

Everyone knew there were large bats in the rainforest, but not one large enough to be considered a monster.

"Have you ever heard of a bat-like monster in Brazil?" Bruce asked Ms. Pantozzi.

"Nope. Just the one in Gotham City," she said with a smirk. "And Batman's not even really a monster."

"Take good notes for me," Bruce said. "I'm going to talk to the protesters."

Ms. Panzotti nodded. Bruce slid out through the audience and exited through the back door of the auditorium.

Outside, security personnel and police officers were loading the protesters into police cars. Scanning the crowd, Bruce noticed that the woman who cried out about the bat monster wasn't among them.

Bruce walked past a protester being led to the police van by an officer. "I'm looking for one of the protesters," Bruce told the policeman. "The woman who talked about the bat monster."

The officer shrugged.

"You mean Erica?" an arrested protester asked. "She escaped into the rainforest. You'll never be able to find her now. Lately it's like people just disappear in there."

"Do you know about the so-called bat monster?" Bruce asked the protester.

"Yeah, of course. But why should I tell you?" the protester snarled. "All you want to do is destroy the rainforest."

"I can help," Bruce said. "But only if you let me."

The protester's expression softened a little.

Bruce could tell the man wanted to believe him.

"The bat monster first showed up a few weeks ago," the protester admitted. "Right after the big construction project started in our village in the rainforest. At first, it would appear out of the shadows, then some of the construction workers would disappear. We guessed they were taken by the bat monster. But then it started taking random men from our village. Erica's husband was one of the ones who disappeared."

The police officer started pushing the protester into the van. "None of this would have happened if people like you hadn't decided to destroy the rainforest with your terrible construction projects," the protester said. "People are disappearing, and so is the rainforest! And despite all your money, people like you can't help with any of it."

The police officer shut the door on the van. A moment later, the van carrying the protesters was gone.

Bruce stared into the rainforest. The protester was probably right. Bruce Wayne probably wouldn't be able to help.

But Batman could.

CHAPTER 2

# BATS

Erica moved quickly through the rainforest toward her village. It was the middle of the day, but the trees were so large and full that it was nearly as dark as night.

She was glad she hadn't gotten arrested with the other protesters, especially since she hadn't actually been protesting like them. She was just desperate to find her husband, Godofredo, and had been looking for help.

As a little girl, Erica had heard the legends of the bat monsters. They were supposedly human-sized bats that would terrorize villages to protect their own homes in the rainforest.

The bat monsters stole villagers, one by one, until everyone had disappeared. Then they would take over the empty village and make it their new home.

Erica never really believed in the bat monsters. Until now.

Until she witnessed one take Godofredo away from her.

**RUSTLE RUSTLE!**

Erica heard something moving in the trees near her. She stopped and looked to her sides, then glanced up above.

Nothing was there. "It's probably just my imagination playing tricks on me," she said to herself, continuing on.

AHHHHH!
YOU ARE THE BAT MONSTER!!
CALM DOWN. I'M NOT GOING TO HURT YOU.

Erica screamed and tried to pull away from Batman.

"Please," Batman said. "I'm not a monster. I'm here to help."

"But you are a giant bat," Erica cried. "You took my husband!"

Batman stepped away from Erica, into a shaft of sunlight that shone through the trees. The light illuminated his face and mask.

Erica's eyes went wide. "You're . . . you're human," she whispered.

Batman nodded and stepped out of the sun. "I dress like this to frighten those who would do evil. I'm called Batman where I come from, but I'm not the bat monster. I've come to find your husband and the others that the bat monster took."

Erica gazed wide-eyed at Batman. Maybe it was the way he spoke, or the sound of his voice. For some reason, Erica believed him.

She turned away from Batman.

"Godofredo is gone forever," she said. "When the bat monster takes people, they are never heard from again. There's nothing you or anyone else can do."

Tears fell from Erica's eyes. She wiped them as she spoke. "Every day, another man from our village is taken from the work site," she said. "Sometimes two men are taken. It happens as day turns to night. The bat monster emerges from the shadows, just like you did. And then it disappears just as quickly with one or more of our villagers."

Batman stepped close to Erica, his protective instincts kicking in. It was almost dusk. If the pattern held true, the monster would appear shortly.

"I will find them," Batman said. "And I will stop the monster."

Erica turned to respond to Batman, but he was gone.

A SHORT TIME LATER...

It had been a long day of labor for João and his fellow workers at the construction site. They'd made a lot of progress on clearing out the trees and other vegetation in this area of the rainforest.

João didn't know what building they were creating, but destroying so much of the rainforest made him miserable. But he had to earn money somehow, and this was the only option for him.

João and a couple of his coworkers were all who remained at the site. The others had gone home early because they were scared of the bat monster.

João was scared as well, but had to clean up all the tools he'd used before he could go home. He was hurrying as fast as he could, but the sun was rapidly disappearing below the horizon.

When all the tools were packed and stored, João and his coworkers began the long trek back home to their village.

LET'S GET MOVING. WE HAVE TO GET HOME BEFORE DARK.
IT CAN'T BE...
SKREEEEE
THE BAT MONSTER!!

João froze.

**SWOOOOOOOSH!**

The bat monster flew toward him at incredible speed. João was certain he was doomed.

"No! Please don't take me!" João yelled at the creature.

**SKREEEEEEEEEE!**

In response, it screamed a terrifying call.

Across the construction site, Batman watched from his tree. His suspicions were right.

*It's Man-Bat,* he realized.

Batman leapt from his tree. He ran with incredible quickness toward the site. Though Batman was closer to the site than Man-Bat had been, Man-Bat could fly faster than Batman could run. It was a race. Batman pulled his high-powered grapnel gun from his Utility Belt.

**FOOSH!**

He blasted it toward João. The bat-shaped hook and its rope hurled toward João, then wrapped around him. Batman yanked on the rope, pulling João to the ground. Man-Bat swooped over João, narrowly missing him.

Batman freed João from the rope as Man-Bat set his sights on a different construction worker. It landed on the ground in front of its new prey. It spread its wings wide. The construction worker tripped over his own feet and fell to the ground. Man-Bat loomed menacingly over him.

"Pedro! We've got to help him!" João yelled. Batman pulled João to his feet.

"Let's go," Batman ordered.

Batman and João raced toward the monster. João grabbed a branch from the ground, swinging it wildly. Batman had a plan.

SMACK!
HELP ME!
THWIP!

Batman glared skyward and watched Man-Bat fly away.

João was furious. "You let him take Pedro!" he cried.

"I'll get him back," Batman said calmly. He showed João a small handheld screen. In the center of the display, a red light flashed.

"I put a tracking device on him," Batman said. "This ends tonight."

CHAPTER 3

# RAINFOREST THROUGH THE TREES

Man-Bat carried Pedro over the trees of the dense rainforest. It was nearing night. Pedro felt a chill in the air. Sure, he was cold — but also terrified. After all, he'd heard of his friends being trapped — or worse — by the bat monster.

Pedro struggled with all his might to try to get free from the monster's claws, but it was no use. The monster was strong. *Very* strong. And even if he did break free, he'd drop to the ground from the sky and hit lots of tree branches on the way down.

Soon, though, the monster descended.

**WOOOSH!**

Man-Bat darted between the thick branches in the rainforest. Then he landed softly on the ground. He threw Pedro down in front of a doorway. It led to a large structure that appeared to be made entirely of plants.

Pedro shuddered. "Where am I?" he cried. "What is this place?"

Man-Bat ignored his questions and stepped toward the entrance. He disappeared into the plant structure.

Pedro stood, a mix of fear and curiosity on his face. Then, with no other choice, he followed Man-Bat inside.

Pedro's eyes darted around. The structure was an impressive web of vines, leaves, and flowers. Then he saw Man-Bat hanging from the plants and branches that formed the ceiling.

Giant leaves blocked out the sky. The darkness was lit only by eerie glowing plants and flowers.

Cast in the ghostly light of these strange plants, Pedro saw people tied to the walls by the vines! He saw a few of his friends from the construction site.

*There is Marcos,* Pedro thought. *And Godofredo!*

Pedro turned to leave as fast as he could, but his feet wouldn't move. There was something holding them.

He looked down. A strong vine was wrapped around his ankle! Another vine snaked slowly from the structure, wrapping around Pedro's arm. A third wound tightly around his waist.

He struggled. Desperately, he tried to pull away from the vines that were growing tighter around his body.

"Help!" he yelled. Then a giant leaf slapped across his mouth, gagging him.

The vines tightened and dragged him toward the wall. His struggling was useless. He was trapped, held captive by impossibly strong, rope-like vines.

His eyes danced around the structure in panic. There were dozens of prisoners like him hanging on the walls.

**POOF!**

Suddenly a cloud of pink dust wafted toward his face, stinging his nose and eyes. He tried to sneeze, but the leaf covering his mouth wouldn't let him. The pink dust lingered for a moment. Then it dissipated.

Pedro didn't need to sneeze anymore, but he couldn't keep his eyes open, either. His eyelids became heavy. A few seconds later, he was unconscious — another silent prisoner of the bat monster.

MEANWHILE...

BLEEP!

BLEEP!

Batman followed the beacon on his tracking monitor. Man-Bat had the luxury of flying over the trees, but Batman was forced to follow his foe on foot through the rainforest. He didn't know the area, and it was dark, so he used the night-vision goggles underneath his cowl to find his way.

Batman was getting closer. *Only a couple more miles to go,* he thought. He wished he had the Batwing with him so he could reach Man-Bat's hideout faster by flying over the trees.

**GRRRROARRRR...**

Batman paused for a moment to listen carefully. The sounds of the rainforest were plentiful, but the low growl of a skulking predator was distinct among the other noises. He heard it again. And again.

Behind him. Above, in a tree. He couldn't see it yet, but it was there.

"Where are you?" Batman whispered as he glanced around his surroundings.

**GRRRRRRRRR...**

The predator growled again. *A jaguar,* he realized.

The jaguar pounced from the trees above. Before Batman could react, he felt something slam into his back and pin him facedown on the ground. Batman slipped an elbow out and pushed the beast off him to the side.

The jaguar leapt backward. Batman got to his feet just in time for the jaguar to pounce again. But this time, Batman was ready. He rolled back and used his foot to flip the heavy feline over his head. The jaguar landed with a thud, but immediately sprang back to its feet and charged full speed at Batman.

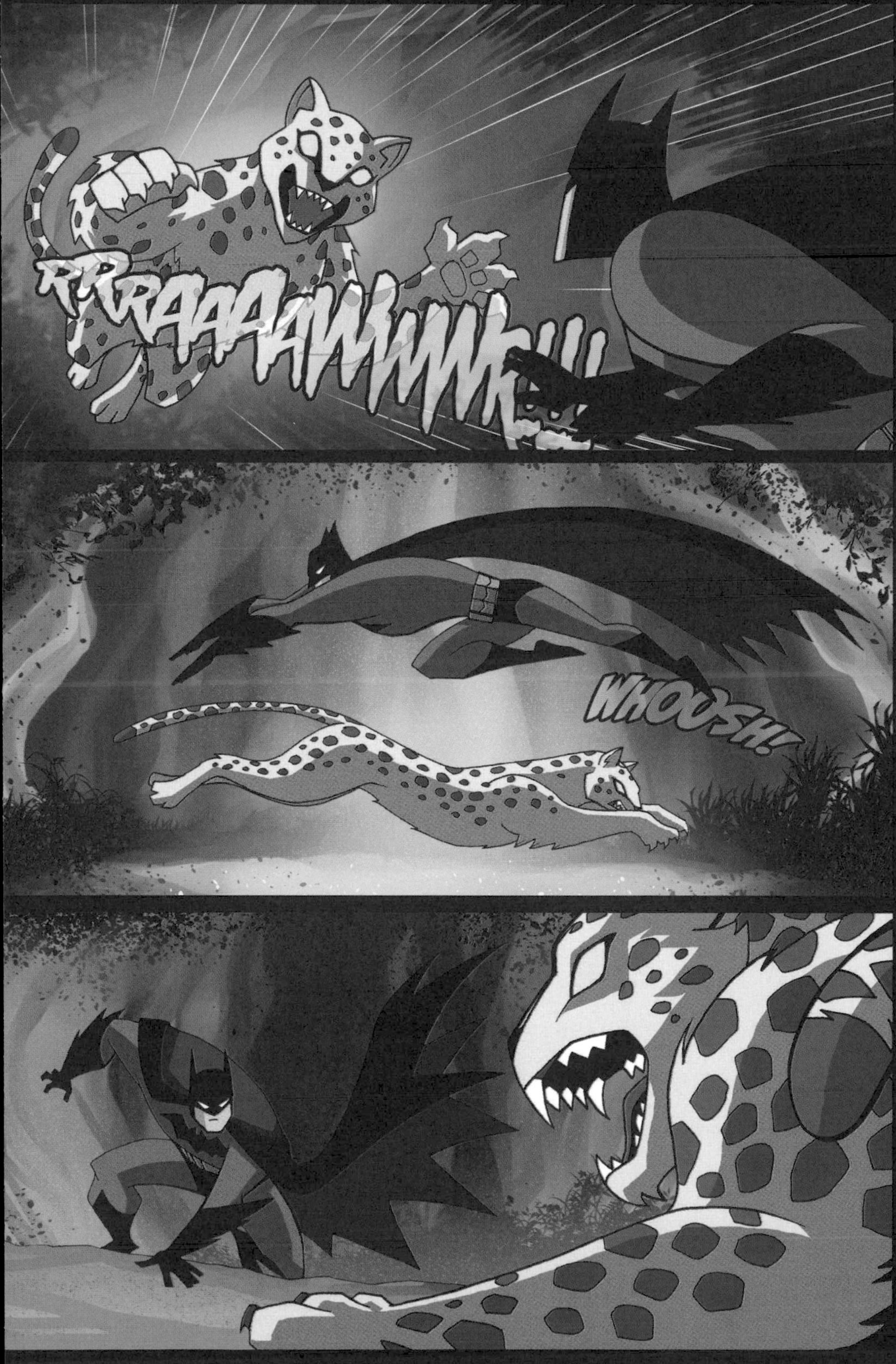
RRRAAAAWWWRR!!!
WHOOSH!

The jaguar was surprisingly agile. Batman knew big cats like this were powerful, but he was surprised at how nimble the jaguar was.

It sprung up the trunk of a tree, then flipped backward off the trunk. Batman rolled out of the way.

The jaguar charged at Batman and swung a claw at him.

**SWOOOSH!**

Batman twisted out of the way, but the claw snagged Batman's cape and tore a small section of it to ribbons. Batman yanked his cape behind him, the ribbon-like section flapping in the wind.

The jaguar backed up, putting some space between itself and Batman. However, this space was to allow the jaguar to build more momentum for its next attack.

This fight was lasting too long.

Batman whipped out a device from his Utility Belt. He pressed the trigger as the jaguar dashed toward Batman. The device sent out a mist that hit the jaguar right in the face.

**FSSSSSHHHHT!**

**GRRRRRRRR!**

The jaguar jerked back from Batman, then began to stumble. The jaguar lay on its side. In a few moments, it was asleep. The knockout gas did the trick, thankfully.

Now Batman could resume his quest to find the Man-Bat and the hostages.

The tracking device showed that soon the trees would be too dense to travel through on foot. He climbed up a nearby tree and scouted the scene ahead. Sure enough, the land ahead was too cluttered to travel by foot.

TIME TO TAKE FLIGHT.
FWIP

With the Batarang firmly attached to a huge tree branch, Batman soared through the air at amazing speed.

**FWIP!**

**SWOOSH!**

**FWIP!**

**SWOOSH!**

As he swung on the rope from tree to tree, his cape flapped in the wind. Swing by swing, he drew closer and closer to the signal coming from the tracking device he'd attached to Man-Bat.

Within minutes, he reached the trees that surrounded the structure where the Man-Bat had gone. He dropped from the trees, landing in front of the entrance to the structure.

WOW.

CHAPTER 4

# PLANT PALACE

Batman saw that it was covered with plants. The tracking device showed that Man-Bat was inside. But as Batman stepped closer, he realized the building wasn't covered with plants — it was built with them! Careful and intricate design had gone into creating the structure out of vines, flowers, and trees.

Batman knew Man-Bat hadn't built this place. This was far too complicated for him to have constructed. That meant he wasn't working alone. And there was only one person in the world who would create a superstructure out of living plants.

Poison Ivy. It all made sense now. The rainforest was made up of lush vegetation and rare animals. Poison Ivy had spent her life trying to protect plants from what she thought was the destructive force of mankind.

In fact, Batman had encountered her in the rainforest before. Just like last time, the rainforest was being continually damaged by development and construction. Too many plants were being killed by men. So Ivy struck back.

It seemed her plan was bigger this time. She needed someone to be the "muscle" in her scheme. She must've used the Man-Bat to attack the humans who were attacking her beloved plants.

She wasn't totally wrong, Batman knew. The rainforest needed to be protected. It was why Bruce Wayne and Ms. Pantozzi had come to Brazil in the first place. They had hoped to sponsor an agreement with the other world economic powers that would have added more protections for the rainforest.

They wanted to prevent the damage being done by mankind's footprints. But Poison Ivy wanted to remove the feet that made the human footprints — all of them. Except her own, of course.

There was still time for Bruce and Ms. Pantozzi's plan, of course, but the bigger problem right now was to rescue the hostages Ivy and Man-Bat had taken. That was where Poison Ivy had gone wrong. Threatening or harming innocent people who were just trying to take care of their families was wrong, even if it was done in order to protect the rainforest.

Using Man-Bat made sense, too. Giant bats thrived in Brazil. They were everywhere. Some bats grew to be almost as big as Man-Bat, though they weren't humanlike like Man-Bat was.

But the legend of the bat monster made the local villagers believe that Man-Bat was really the monster they'd heard so much about. And since Poison Ivy could control any man she wanted by manipulating plant pheromones,

Man-Bat was the perfect choice to help her in her nefarious plan. All she'd had to do was work her magic with the pheromones, and he fell into her power.

She had to be stopped.

Batman entered the plant structure. There were dozens of hostages covered in vines and leaves. They looked like plant-mummies lining the walls of the massive structure.

"Ivy! I know you're here!" Batman called out. "Stop hiding and face me!"

From high above Batman, several vines dropped from the ceiling. A platform made of giant leaves lowered to the ground. Poison Ivy stood on the platform as it descended down the vines like an elevator on cables.

"Hello, Batman," Poison Ivy said, her voice thick with disgust.

"Release these prisoners," Batman ordered.

Poison Ivy laughed. "I don't think I'm going to be doing that," she said. She snapped her fingers. The vines sprang to action.

NOW PLEASE EXCUSE ME...
...I HAVE A RAINFOREST TO SAVE.
NOT TODAY.

Batman glared at Poison Ivy. His patience was growing thin.

"If I let them go, they'll just start killing the rainforest again," Poison Ivy explained matter-of-factly. "And I simply can't let that happen. I won't let that happen. In fact, I'm not going to stop until there's no one left to disturb Mother Nature's handiwork."

Poison Ivy leapt off the leaf-elevator and landed a few feet from Batman. She approached one of the prisoners, wrapped in the vines on the wall, and caressed his face.

"Batman, you can't stop me," she said. "I control the plants, and the rainforest is full of them! They are my family. And I'd do anything to protect my family."

She walked toward Batman and drew close to him. A sly, devious smile passed over her lips. "Anything," she whispered.

**POOF!**

Poison Ivy raised her hands to her lips and blew a cloud of pink powder at Batman's face.

Poison Ivy glared at him. "Go to sleep, Batman," she said.

Batman glared at Poison Ivy. "No," he growled.

Poison Ivy stepped backward, shocked that her powder hadn't knocked Batman out cold. "What?! How —? Why didn't that work?!" she screamed.

"I was ready for you this time, Ivy," Batman said.

**TAP!**

**TAP!**

**TAP!**

Batman tapped on a transparent shield around his nose and mouth. "Your charms don't work on me," Batman said with a grin.

Ivy balled up her fists at her sides and screamed, "Get him!"

Batman yanked his arms hard toward his Utility Belt. The resistance from the vines that were wrapping around him was stronger than he'd anticipated. But he pulled and pulled until his right hand reached his belt.

# CLICK!

He produced a Batarang from his belt just as two more vines wrapped around his wrists. They pulled his arms farther and farther away from his belt.

Batman tightened his grip on the Batarang. Using all of the strength in his arms he could muster, he flicked his wrist. The Batarang flew upward at one of the sets of vines that was gripping his left arm.

**KIRSH!**

Its razor-sharp edge sliced through the vines like they were made of thin thread.

Poison Ivy cried out as if in pain. "You'll pay for that, Batman!" she shrieked.

With his free left arm, Batman snapped the vines that held his right arm and then he tore away the other vines holding him back. He was free! Poison Ivy leapt back onto her plant elevator. It lifted her up to her hiding place at the top of the lair.

Before Batman could chase after her or free the hostages, a dark shadow fell over him from above. He looked up. Man-Bat was sailing toward him at tremendous speed.

**THUMP!**

Man-Bat collided with Batman. The human bat wrapped his claws around Batman's arms and flew toward the ceiling. Man-Bat flapped his wings faster and harder to build up speed.

FWOOOSH!

The ceiling of the plant structure sped toward them. Batman wrestled against Man-Bat's claws, twisting and turning to get free. He strained every muscle in his body against Man-Bat's grip. But it was no use.

CRUNCH!

Man-Bat and Batman burst through the leaves, vines, branches, and flowers that made up the ceiling. Both of them were dazed by the impact.

Man-Bat chaotically flew into the night sky with Batman in tow. The plants they tore a hole through were instantly replaced by other plants. In a matter of moments, the hole in the building was repaired.

With great effort, Batman was finally able

to apply enough force to pry open Man-Bat's claws. Batman climbed onto Man-Bat's back and held on to his neck so he wouldn't fall to his death.

Man-Bat spun around in a barrel roll to shake Batman off his back, but Batman held tight.

**SLAP!**

**SLAP!**

Man-Bat tried swatting at Batman with his wings, but it was no use. He couldn't reach, and the more he tried, the slower his flight became. He and Batman were starting to fall from the sky.

Man-Bat shifted his body until it was heading straight down. He tucked his wings. Batman could feel his hands slipping as the wind from the rocket-like divebomb smashed into him. So Batman dug his fingers into Man-Bat's shoulders.

**SKREEEEEEEEE!**

Man-Bat let out a shrill cry of pain. Batman swung his leg up on Man-Bat's back and kicked Man-Bat's forearm on his wing.

**WHUMP!**

The blow forced Man-Bat to extend his wing, stopping the dive.

Batman drove his elbow into Man-Bat's shoulder.

**THUMP!**

Man-Bat leveled off his flight, and again flapped his wings while Batman clung to his back.

Poison Ivy's plant palace loomed large below them. Batman was determined to ground Man-Bat before he could get back inside. Otherwise, there was no way he'd rescue the hostages.

ENOUGH OF THIS, MAN-BAT.
WOOOOOOSH!!
CRACKK!!

Batman raced over to Man-Bat's unconscious body. He pulled a small handheld air injection device from his Utility Belt and pressed it into Man-Bat's shoulder.

SWIRSH!

Batman removed the injection gun. "The antidote will take a while to work," he said to the disoriented Man-Bat. "Until it does, you'll be unconscious. Once I free those hostages, I'll get you into custody. We'll make sure you're back to normal soon, Dr. Langstrom."

Batman used some steel cable from the Batrope to secure Man-Bat to the tree until he could come back for him. The combination of the antidote and the Batrope would be enough to keep Man-Bat safe until he returned to his human form.

Now it was time to stop Poison Ivy.

CHAPTER 5

# THE RESCUE

A SHORT WHILE LATER...

Batman reentered Poison Ivy's compound. It was quiet. *Too* quiet. Batman didn't see Poison Ivy anywhere, but knew she was hiding nearby, waiting to strike. Whenever she did, he'd be ready.

In the meantime, though, he had a job to do: free the hostages.

Batman approached one of the men tied to the wall. Using a Batarang, he began to cut the vines that held this first hostage.

**SLICE!**

**SLICE!**

Batman pulled the loose vines away from the hostage, and tore sticky leaves from his body. Soon, the hostage was free. It was Pedro. The weakened man gasped for air and fell into Batman's arms.

"You saved me," Pedro said between gasps.

"Yes," Batman said. "And I'm going to save the others. But I need your help."

Batman handed Pedro a second Batarang. "Start cutting vines off your friends. We don't have much time. Poison Ivy will soon figure out what we're doing, and she won't like it."

Pedro nodded. He raced to one of the other hostages. Soon he and Batman were making great progress in freeing the hostages.

As the hostages were broken out of the plant cocoons they'd been trapped in, they fell to the ground, weak, hungry, and dehydrated. They were happy they'd been freed, though, and after regaining their bearings, helped Batman and Pedro continue cutting down other captives.

"Get out of here," Batman said to the freed hostages. "Go back to your homes. Quickly, before it's too late!"

The newly freed hostages made their way to the exit.

**SHIRRRRSH!**

**KRICH!**

Several giant trees moved and twisted around each other to block the door with their branches. The hostages huddled together, unable to exit.

"You're not going anywhere, boys," Poison Ivy said as she slid down the twisted trees.

**POOF!**

Poison Ivy spread the pink knockout dust over the group of hostages, sending them back to an unconscious state. They slumped down on top of one another, collapsing in a pile of humanity.

Poison Ivy turned to Batman. "You just don't get it!" she snarled. "If we destroy Mother Earth and her wonderful creations, then there will be nothing left!"

"No, Ivy, *you* don't get it," Batman said calmly. "Harming people and their families is not the way to get your message out to the rest of the world. Violence isn't the answer."

"They're casualties of war, Batman," Poison Ivy said. Her voice grew louder with each comment. "Saving the Earth is worth losing a few dozen of her enemies. More, even. You have hurt too many plants tonight already. I saw you butchering my sweet saplings as you took my hostages away. But now they will have their revenge — through me! Prepare to feel the pain you caused my plants!"

ATTACK!
SLICE

Batman shook his head. "Give up, Ivy. You can't win."

"Watch me," Ivy said.

Poison Ivy directed more vines and plants at Batman, but he would not be captured!

**SWOOSH!**
**FWIRSH!**
**SWISH-SLICE-SWISH!**

Batman dodged, weaved, and sliced his way through and between the growing and attacking plant life.

**THUMP!**

A thick tree trunk burst from the ground, shooting toward the ceiling. Batman leapt onto the growing tree and rode it up to the top of the structure. The treetop slammed into the ceiling.

**CRUNCH!**

It broke another hole through the leafy top of the compound. Batman placed a small explosive charge on the ceiling near the top of the tree. Then he grabbed onto a vine that had woven throughout the ceiling, and swung hand over hand across it.

One by one, Batman placed more explosive charges along the ceiling.

"What are you doing?!" Poison Ivy screamed at the top of her lungs.

Batman silently cut another vine free from the ceiling and rappelled down the side of the structure with it.

"Stop it!" Poison Ivy shrieked. "You're not supposed to hurt the plants! Stop hurting the plants!"

Batman continued, ignoring her. Ivy sent more plants to attack him, but he again avoided them.

**FWISH!**
**ZIP!**

Batman jumped and flipped out of the way. The plants tied themselves together in a messy knot of vines.

The Caped Crusader moved close to the pile of unconscious hostages. Nearby, he began cutting an opening with a Batarang that would function as a doorway.

"No!" Poison Ivy screeched again. She commanded more giant leaves to lunge at Batman. "Grab him!"

As the giant leaves and vines surged at Batman, he got into position in front of the hostages and the doorway — and waited. Just before the leaves and vines were upon him, he dived to the side.

The leaves surrounded the unconscious hostages until they were fully, loosely, wrapped in the leaves. For now, they were shielded from the rest of the building.

Batman took his Batarang with a rope attached and wrapped it around the leaves, securing the leaves around the hostages.

The leaves were extra thick and strong. As Batman predicted, Poison Ivy had made them that way so he wouldn't be able to cut through them. Instead, they would protect the hostages from what would happen next.

"This is your last warning, Ivy," Batman said. "Give up."

Poison Ivy climbed up a small tree and stood on a branch. She motioned around her, taking in the structure with her hands. "Why would I do that, Batman?" she cried. "This is my kingdom! I control these plants. I protect these plants. They are my family. And no one is going to stop me or take them away from me! Not you. Not any deforesting construction company. No one!"

Batman sighed. He pulled a remote from his Utility Belt and pressed a small button on it.

CLICK!

"You have ten seconds, Ivy," Batman said. "Give up, or it all ends."

Poison Ivy sneered at Batman. "No."

BEEP! BEEP! BEEP!
BEEP! BEEP! BEEP!
BOOM!
BOOM!
BOOM!
GET DOWN!
KA-BOOOOM!

As the charges exploded, Batman pulled Poison Ivy to safety.

LATER...

A massive police and rescue team arrived at the site of the collapsed plant structure. Medical helicopters were evacuating and caring for the freed hostages. It took several police crews using saws to cut open the entwined, leafy cocoon Batman had created for the hostages. Thankfully none of them were injured. And soon the rainforest would return to its natural state, free from Poison Ivy's influence.

Pedro sat inside one of the medical helicopters while a medic treated him. "How did you find us?" Pedro asked.

"We received your coordinates and directions from an anonymous source," the medic replied.

"It was Batman," Pedro said.

The nurse looked confused. "You mean the bat monster? No, I don't think so," she said. "The monster is being taken into custody."

Pedro shook his head and smiled. He knew Batman had saved them before disappearing. He glanced out the window of the helicopter. Police officers were loading Man-Bat and Poison Ivy into a secure helicopter to be airlifted out of the area and to prison.

Man-Bat was wrapped in several giant, thick chains. His wings were secured to his body so he couldn't fly away. Poison Ivy wore a straightjacket and had her mouth covered with a strap so she couldn't control the nearby plants in order to escape.

After they were loaded inside, the chopper lifted skyward, leaving the rubble of the area behind.

The medical helicopters floated upward, carrying the former hostages to safety, away from the plant prison that had held them captive. They were finally free.

THAT EVENING...

Erica heard the rumble of a car engine outside her small home on the outskirts of the rainforest. She raced to the door to see who it was. Her heart jumped as she saw her beloved husband, Godofredo, climb out of a police car.

Erica ran to her husband as fast as she could. The couple grabbed each other in a big, tight embrace.

"I thought I'd lost you forever," Erica said, tears filling her eyes.

"I thought so, too," Godofredo said, wiping his own away. "The bat monster took me."

"I know," Erica said. "But it was Batman who saved you."

Godofredo nodded.

In the shadows of the rainforest near Erica and Godofredo's home, Batman watched the joyous reunion take place.

As Erica and Godofredo walked back into their home, Batman stepped further into the shadows. The Dark Knight's work here was finished. But Bruce Wayne had one final matter to take care of . . .

Ms. Pantozzi was prepared. She had come to Brazil to give a speech with Bruce Wayne, and it was time to begin.

Ms. Pantozzi didn't know how her speech would be received by the influential audience members. Truthfully, she didn't care. After all, their purpose was important. As long as the economic delegates agreed to participate in the plan, they didn't have to like it.

Bruce peeked out from the side of the stage at the large audience. He had a hard time reading their expressions and reactions, though more than a few seemed a little skeptical. They had their work cut out for them.

Bruce approached Ms. Pantozzi backstage. "Shall we?" Bruce said.

"Let's," Ms. Pantozzi said.

"After you," Bruce said.

Ms. Pantozzi smiled and entered the stage, followed by billionaire Bruce Wayne.

BRUCE WAYNE AND MS. PANTOZZI TAKE THE STAGE.
WAYNE ENTERPRISES
MY FRIENDS, WE HAVE GATHERED THIS WEEK TO DISCUSS WHAT WE CAN DO TO BETTER PROTECT THE RAINFOREST.
WAYNE ENTERPRISES IS PLEASED TO ANNOUNCE THAT WE ARE SHUTTING DOWN ALL PROJECTS THAT CAUSE HARM TO THE ENVIRONMENT HERE.
ADDITIONALLY, ALL WAYNE ENTERPRISE'S EMPLOYEES WHO WERE WORKING HERE WILL BE GIVEN NEW JOBS FIXING THE RAINFOREST.

Suddenly, in the back of the auditorium, one person stood and began clapping her hands. Then another. Then a few more. Soon, the entire auditorium was standing and clapping in support of their pledge to protect the planet.

Ms. Pantozzi smiled at Bruce. "Nice work, Mr. Wayne," she said.

He winked. "I only played a small part in this," he said.

THE NEXT DAY...

As he boarded the plane to return home to Gotham City, Bruce looked across the vastness of the rainforest. He knew the plan would cost his company a lot of money, but he didn't care. He was proud of everything he had accomplished. The citizens of the world were now safe from Poison Ivy and Man-Bat. And Ms. Pantozzi and Wayne Enterprises had created a better way to protect the planet.

Everybody won in the Wayne Enterprises plan. Especially the planet. And that was the sweetest victory of all.

# POISON IVY

**REAL NAME:**
Pamela Isley

**OCCUPATION:**
Botanist, Criminal

**BASE:**
Gotham City

**HEIGHT:**
5 feet 6 inches

**WEIGHT:**
110 pounds

**EYES:**
Green

**HAIR:**
Auburn

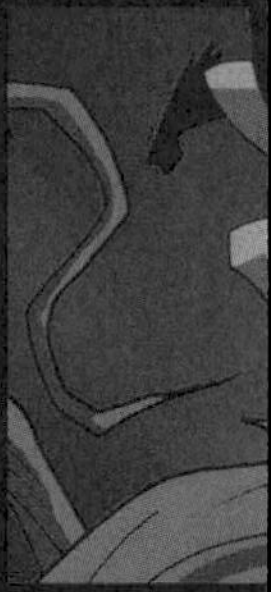

Pamela Isley was born with immunities to plant toxins and poisons. Her love of plants began to grow like a weed at an early age. She eventually became a botanist, or plant scientist. Through reckless experimentation with various flora, Pamela Isley's skin itself has become poisonous. Her venomous lips and plant weapons present a real problem for crime fighters. But Ivy's most dangerous quality is her extreme love of nature — she cares more about the smallest seed than any human.

- Poison Ivy was once engaged to Gotham City's District Attorney, Harvey Dent, who eventually became the super-villain Two-Face! Their relationship ended when Dent built a prison on a field of wildflowers.
- Poison Ivy emits toxic fragrances that can be harmful to humans. Whenever she is locked up in Arkham Asylum, a wall of Plexiglas must separate her from the guards to ensure their safety.
- Ivy may love her plant creations, but that love hasn't always been returned. A man-eating plant of her own design became self-aware, or sentient. The thing called itself Harvest and turned on Ivy.
- Ivy's connection to plants is so strong that she can control them by thought alone.

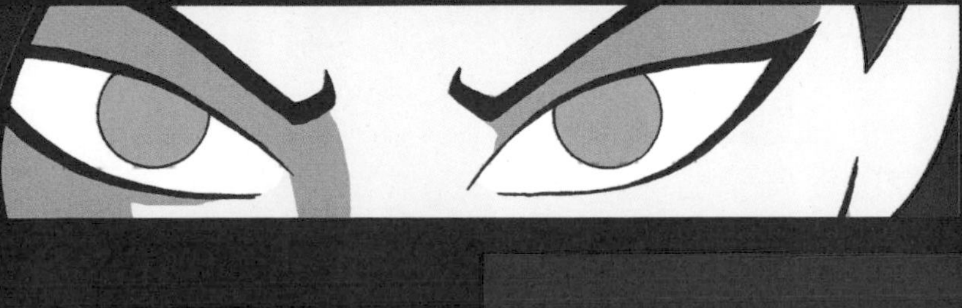

# BIOGRAPHIES

**JAKE BLACK** is a prolific writer with more than 400 publishing and production credits to his name in print, TV, DVD, web, and more. He's written for franchises like Batman, Superman, Teenage Mutant Nina Turtles, Adventure Time, Star Trek, and many others. He lives in a quiet town in Utah with his wife, son, and twin daughters.

**LUCIANO VECCHIO** was born in 1982 and currently lives in Buenos Aires, Argentina. With experience in illustration, animation, and comics, his works have been published in the US, Spain, the UK, France, and Argentina. His credits include Ben 10 (DC Comics), Cruel Thing (Norma), Unseen Tribe (Zuda Comics), and Sentinels (Drumfish Productions).

# SKETCHES

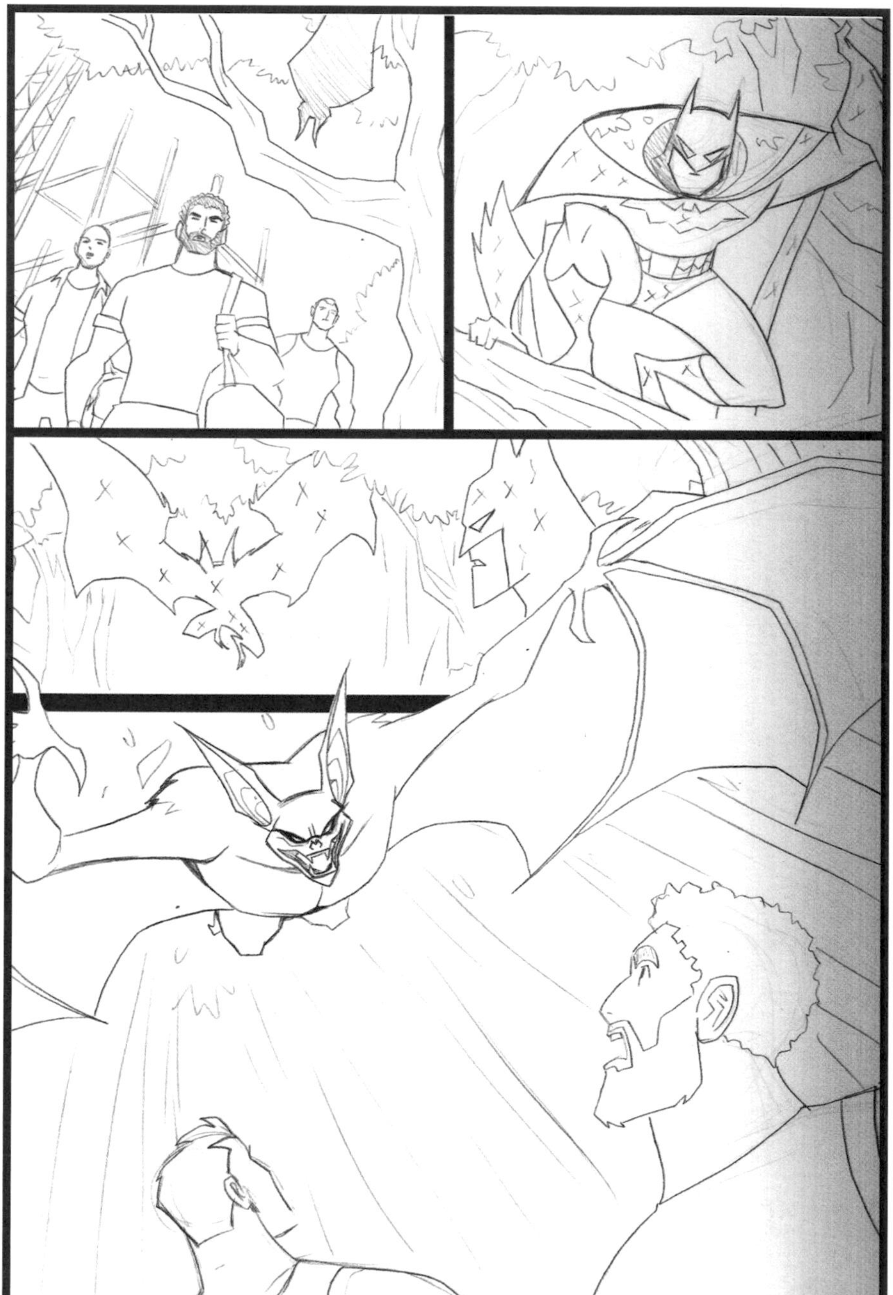

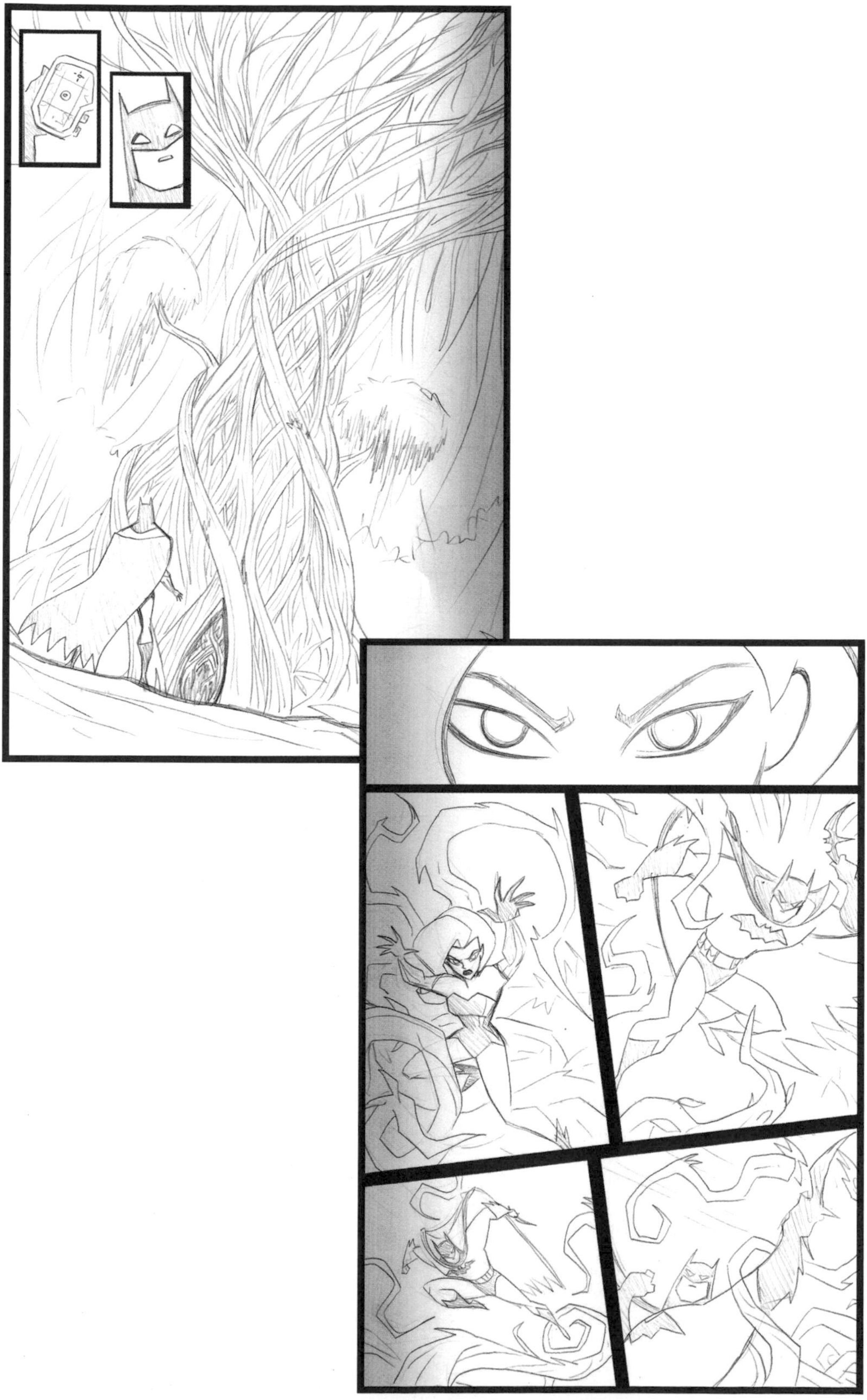

# FINAL ART

SLICE

# COMICS TERMS

**caption** (KAP-shuhn)—words that appear in a box. Captions are often used to set the scene.

**gutter** (GUHT-er)—the space between panels or pages

**motion lines** (MOH-shuhn LINES)—illustrator-created marks that help show motion in art

**panel** (PAN-uhl)—a single drawing that has borders around it. Each panel is a separate scene on a spread.

**SFX** (ESS-EFF-EKS)—short for sound effects. Sound effects are words used to show sounds that occur in the art of a comic.

**splash** (SPLASH)—a large illustration that often covers a full page (or more)

**spread** (SPRED)—two side-by-side pages in a comic book

**word balloon** (WURD BUH-loon)—a speech indicator that includes a character's dialogue or thoughts. A word balloon's tail leads to the speaking character's mouth.

# GLOSSARY

**Batarang** (BAT-uh-rang)—a boomerang-like projectile Batman often uses in battle

**cluttered** (KLUHT-erd)—a large amount of things that are not arranged in a neat or orderly way

**instincts** (IN-stingktz)—if you use your instincts, you trust your gut to make to decisions

**jaguar** (JAG-wahr)—a large, brown, wild cat with black spots

**posturing** (PAHSS-choor-ing)—behaving in a way intended to impress others

**protest** (PROH-test)—to show or express strong disapproval of something at a public event with other people

**rainforest** (RAYN-fohr-isst)—a tropical forest with tall, densely growing, broad-leaved evergreen trees in an area of high annual rainfall

**terrorize** (TAYR-or-ize)—produce great fear

**Utility Belt** (yoo-TIL-uh-tee BEHLT)—the belt Batman wears that holds his many gadgets and crimefighting tools

# VISUAL QUESTIONS

1. Batman knows his enemies well through research. How does his knowledge of Poison Ivy help him in defeating her? Find as many examples as you can.

2. Why does Bruce pay special attention to this woman's words? What do you think he is thinking?

3. Why do Man-Bat's wings overlap the panel border above? Why do you think the artist did this?

4. What is happening in these two panels to the right? How do you know? Explain your answer.